D0480740

MEET THE CREW

CAPTAIN BANANA BEARD

Captain Banana Beard is the almost brave leader of the monkey pirates. Banana Beard often puts his search for treasure before the safety of his crew. But he always gives credit where credit is due!

FIRST MATE FEZ

Wearing a red fez hat (I wonder how he got his name?), Fez is in charge of the ship's charts and books. He tries to stop Captain Banana Beard's plans from getting too crazy, but that's a nearly impossible job for any monkey!

BANANA JUICE

BANANAS

CREWMAN MR PICKLES

Mr Pickles is the lowest on the chain of command, but he still tries hard to be the best pirate he can be. With every job he does, Mr Pickles is one step closer to being a great pirate captain, just like his hero – Captain Banana Beard.

QUARTERMASTER FOSSEY

Fossey keeps track of the ship's goods and treasure. She's in charge of all the equipment and knows the supplies down to the last banana. And if the adventure calls for a certain tool that the ship doesn't have, Fossey can build it in record time.

COCO nut oil

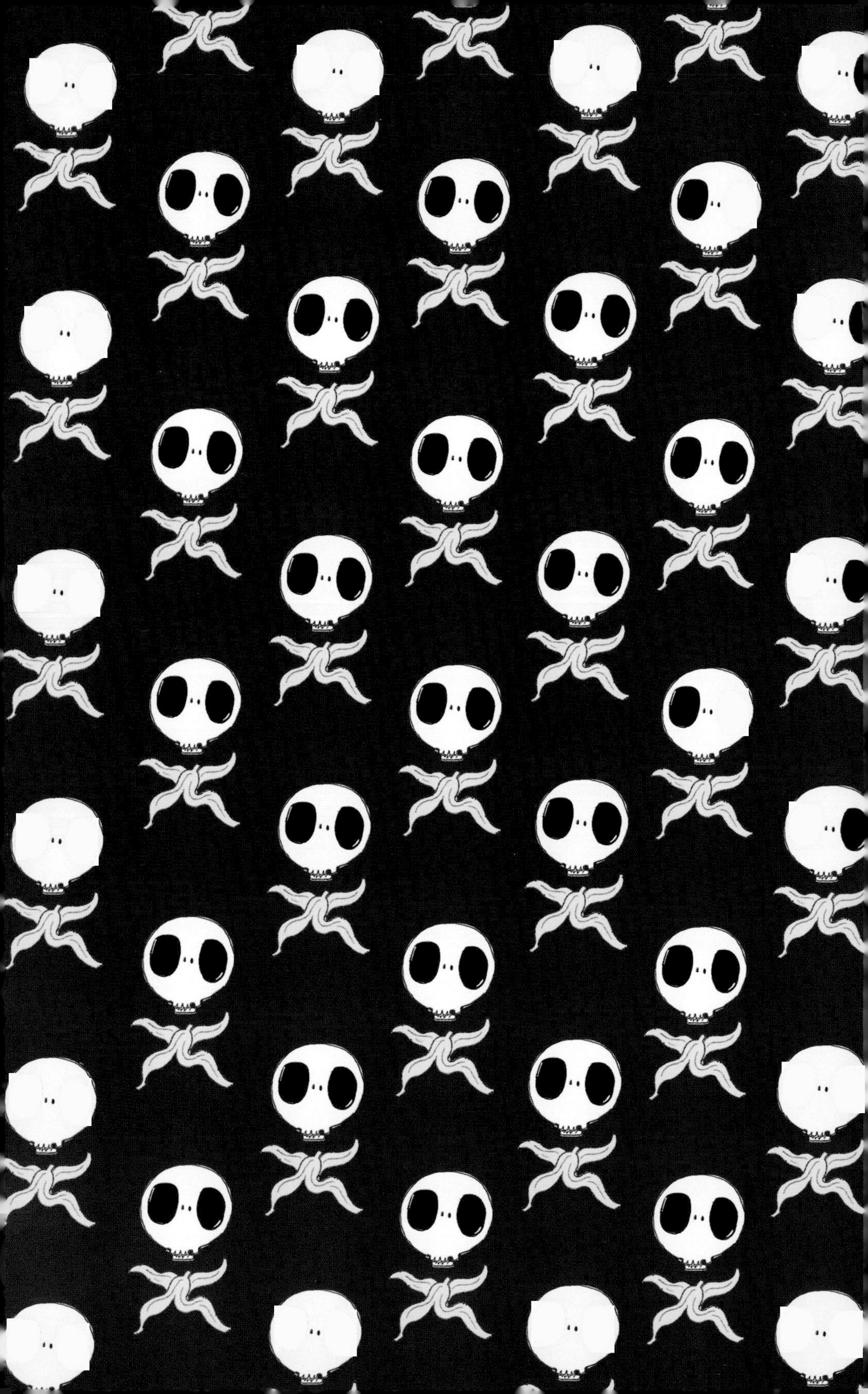

CHAPTER 1

MONKEY PIRATE PRACTICE

"When I'm a monkey pirate captain," Mr Pickles said to himself, "I'll have to draw treasure maps all the time."

The young monkey was drawing with crayons behind two banana barrels. He had made his very own treasure map.

The map showed one large island with two smaller ones.

A large banana-shaped volcano poked out of the big island.

Mr Pickles used a black crayon to add three birds flying high in the sky. Then he drew an X with a red crayon on the large island.

"X marks the spot," Mr Pickles said. "That's where I would bury my treasure."

"Now, see these here?"
he asked.

"Those squiggly lines?"
asked Fossey.

"Aye," replied the captain.
"Those birds be blackleberry
sap-suckers."

"Begging the captain's pardon,"
said Mr Pickles.

"Do be quiet, Mr Pickles," the
captain growled. "That's an order."

Mr Pickles opened his mouth
to reply. Then he closed it. He
couldn't disobey the captain's
orders.

Banana Beard continued.

"Now, the blackleberry sap-sucker flies east at this time of year. So prepare to set sail!" The captain grinned. "East!"

CHAPTER 2

FLYING COCONUTS

"Land ho!" Fossey shouted. That was monkey pirate talk for *I can see some land.*

Mr Pickles couldn't believe his ears. He joined everyone at the front of the ship.

A *real* island poked out of the sea. It had two smaller ones nearby. The big one even had a banana-shaped volcano. They looked just like the islands he had drawn.

"What did I tell you, mateys?"

asked the captain. "There she be.

Our treasure island!"

The monkey pirates took a smaller boat to shore. They found themselves in a thick jungle. Captain Banana Beard led the way. He held the treasure map up.

"This way, mateys," he said. "We'll have that treasure in no time!"

Fez and Fossey marched behind him. Mr Pickles brought up the rear. He carried several shovels.

The jungle was dark and spooky. Mr Pickles felt as if someone or something was watching his every move.

"This is one creepy island," Fossey whispered.

"You said it," Fez agreed.
"I hope it's not far to the – ouch!" A coconut flew off the ground and hit him.

"What's wrong?" asked Fossey.

Fez rubbed his face. "A coconut just hit my chin."

"How did a falling coconut hit your chin?" she asked.

"It didn't fall," replied Fez. "It flew up."

Fossey shook her head. "Coconuts fall down, not– "

She stopped in the middle of her sentence as coconuts flew off the ground around them. The monkey pirates ducked and dodged them.

"What's going on?" asked Fez.

Mr Pickles couldn't take it anymore. He dropped the shovels and ran to the front of the line. He tugged on the captain's coat.

"What is it, Mr Pickles?" asked Banana Beard.

Mr Pickles pointed at himself and then at the map.

The captain rolled his eyes. "Yes, I know. You found the map. I told you 'well done, lad', didn't I?"

Mr Pickles nodded and pointed at the map again.

"Just yo-ho-hold that thought," said the captain. He squinted his eyes. "I must first bow to his majesty, the monkey pirate king, Captain Baggypants the Third."

The captain bowed to the large monkey pirate standing in the jungle ahead of them.

That is, he bowed to the large *glowing* monkey pirate.

"Uh . . . begging the captain's pardon," said Fez, "but Captain Baggypants . . . has been dead for one hundred years."

"That means that he's . . . he's . . . ," began Fossey.

"A ghost!" finished Fez.

CHAPTER 3

THE HAUNTED HUNT

"Who dares set foot on me haunted island?" asked the ghost of Captain Baggypants.

Banana Beard bowed again. "'Tis I. Captain . . . RUN!" He turned and dashed past the others. Fez, Fossey and Mr Pickles hurried after him.

Captain Baggypants scratched his head.